# BAD GUY

HANNAH BARNABY  &  MIKE YAMADA

Simon & Schuster Books for Young Readers

New York  London  Toronto  Sydney  New Delhi

For Freddie Hernaby,
the original bad guy
—H. B.

SIMON & SCHUSTER BOOKS FOR YOUNG READERS • An imprint of Simon & Schuster Children's Publishing Division • 1230 Avenue of the Americas, New York, New York 10020 • Text copyright © 2017 by Hannah Barnaby • Illustrations copyright © 2017 by Mike Yamada • All rights reserved, including the right of reproduction in whole or in part in any form. • SIMON & SCHUSTER BOOKS FOR YOUNG READERS is a trademark of Simon & Schuster, Inc. • For information about special discounts for bulk purchases, please contact Simon & Schuster Special Sales at 1-866-506-1949 or business@simonandschuster.com. • The Simon & Schuster Speakers Bureau can bring authors to your live event. For more information or to book an event, contact the Simon & Schuster Speakers Bureau at 1-866-248-3049 or visit our website at www.simonspeakers.com. • Book design by Chloë Foglia • The text for this book was set in Garamond. • The illustrations for this book were rendered digitally. Manufactured in China • 0217 SCP • First Edition • 2 4 6 8 10 9 7 5 3 1 Library of Congress Cataloging-in-Publication Data • Names: Barnaby, Hannah Rodgers, author. | Yamada, Mike, illustrator. • Title: Bad guy / Hannah Barnaby; illustrated by Mike Yamada. • Description: First edition. | New York : Simon & Schuster Books for Young Readers, [2017] | Summary: A little boy whose mother calls him "Sweetie Pie" and "Buddy Bear" proves he is a bad guy, especially where his little sister is concerned. • Identifiers: LCCN 2015047862 | ISBN 9781481460101 (hardcover : alk. paper) | ISBN 9781481460118 (eBook) • Subjects: | CYAC: Behavior—Fiction. | Brothers and sisters—Fiction. | Family life—Fiction. • Classification: LCC PZ7.B253 Bad 2017 | DDC [E]—dc23 LC record available at https://lccn.loc.gov/2015047862

I am a bad guy.

Alice runs when she sees me coming.

Mom calls me
Sweetie Pie and
Buddy Bear.

But I am not those things.

I am *bad.*

On Monday I trapped all the
superheroes in a giant cage
with a bunch of hungry lions.

On Tuesday I sailed the seven seas
and kept all the treasure for myself.

On Wednesday I swallowed some astronauts whole.

On Thursday I ran the sheriff out of town.

On Friday I ate Alice's brain.

Mom told me to say I was sorry.
But bad guys don't apologize.

On Saturday we went to the library.
I love the library. They have excellent books for bad guys.

I got one about magic tricks, one about tying knots, and a cookbook.

I had big plans.

Alice picked out her own books.
Probably a bunch of unicorn stories.

When we got home, Mom went to work in the garden. "Play nice, you two," she said.

But bad guys don't play nice.

I went to work.

Bad guys work hard. But sometimes . . .

even bad guys
need to take a
Popsicle break.

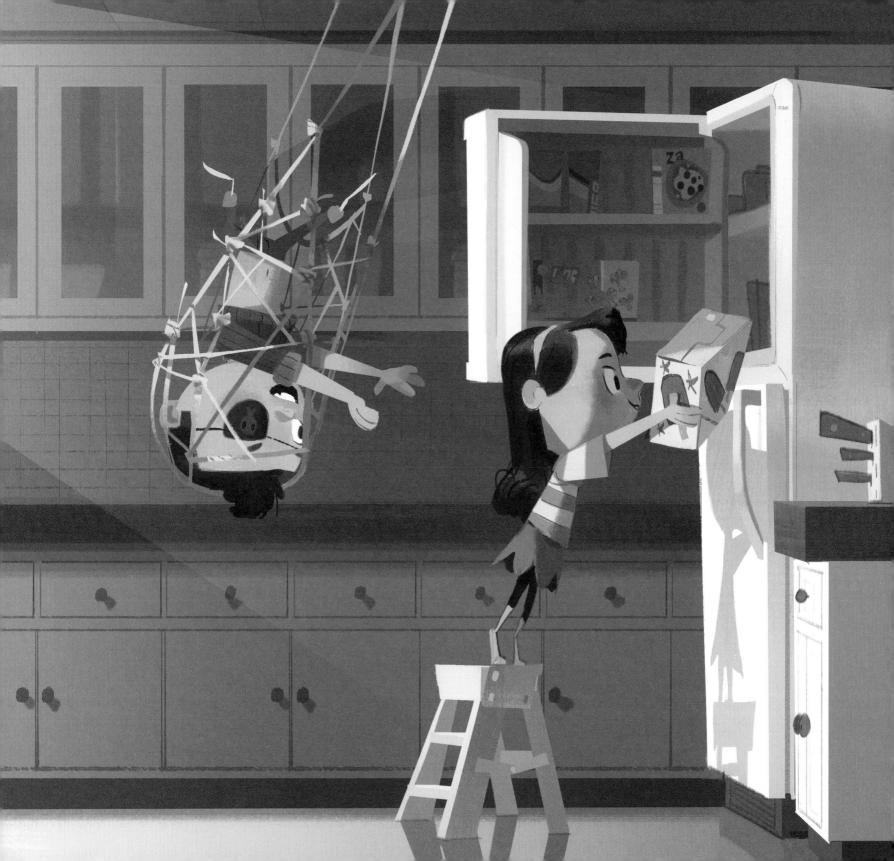

Alice ate all the orange Popsicles right in front of me.

"No fair," I said.

Alice smiled an orange smile and said,
"Not every bad guy is a guy."